Lidia's Family Kitchen

NONNA'S BIRTHDAY SURPRISE

LIDIA BASTIANICH

Illustrated by Renée Graef

RP | KIDS

PHILADELPHIA • LONDON

With much love, I dedicate this book to my mother, Erminia, now 92. Her birthday is the crux of this story, and more importantly, her teachings inspired its message.

My brother and I were blessed to grow up in a home where our meals were effortlessly seasonal because we ate what we could grow. We sometimes took this food for granted as kids, but time has instilled in me a profound appreciation for anyone who works to feed a family well—and that's just how we ate: well. Our meals were never fancy or expensive, but they were thoughtfully crafted from fresh ingredients, with love.

With this book I thank my mother for raising me with an appreciation for the inherent wisdom of nature's rhythms, sharing it all with the family, and for passing down many timeless recipes that truly highlight that wisdom.

Grazie,
Lidia

Books published by Running Press are available at special discounts for bulk purchases
in the United States by corporations, institutions, and other organizations. For more information,
please contact the Special Markets Department at the Perseus Books Group, 2300 Chestnut Street, Suite 200,
Philadelphia, PA 19103, or call (800) 810-4145, ext. 5000, or e-mail special.markets@perseusbooks.com.

ISBN 978-0-7624-4655-1
Library of Congress Control Number: 2012944237

9   8   7   6   5   4   3   2   1
Digit on the right indicates the number of this printing

Back cover photo: Diana DeLucia
Designed by Frances J. Soo Ping Chow
Illustrated by Renée Graef
Edited by Lisa Cheng
Typography: Perpetua, Murray Hill, and Univers

Published by Running Press Kids
An Imprint of Running Press Book Publishers
A Member of the Perseus Books Group
2300 Chestnut Street
Philadelphia, PA 19103-4371

Visit us on the web!
www.runningpress.com
www.lidiasitaly.com

Dear Reader,

Growing up as a young girl in Istria, my happiest memories were about food. Sharing simple, joyful meals with loved ones—also growing, harvesting, and preparing the foods we ate. Almost everything we consumed we grew or raised ourselves. Our lives were in sync with the rhythms of nature—the land, plants, animals, and seasons. We ate what was ripe and fresh in the spring, summer, and fall, and cured, canned, and preserved foods to last us through the winter. We knew where our food came from and respected it, using everything and wasting nothing. As a child, I explored the things I ate—picking, peeling, touching, tasting, and smelling. Food excited all of my senses *and* my mind. Today, I share this joy and respect for food with my own children and grandchildren, who call me Nonni, a version of *Nonna* or "grandma" in Italian. I hope you too will share in the excitement and happiness that comes not just from eating food, but in truly *knowing* and *experiencing* it.

Andy Bostick

"Ah! A special treat on this lovely spring day," Nonni Lidia said as she walked into her kitchen and saw her grandchildren. "Olivia, Lorenzo, Miles, Ethan, and Julia—what brings you all here together?"

"Nonna Mima's birthday," said Olivia.

"We want to surprise her," said Lorenzo.

"With dinner," said Miles.

"A special dinner," said Ethan.

"VERY special," added Julia. Her doll Lucia nodded along.

"What a wonderful idea!" Nonni Lidia said.

Nonni Lidia clapped her hands together. "Okay, chefs. If we are having a dinner we need to plan our menu."

"Cool!" said Lorenzo. "Our own menu. Just like in your restaurants."

"How do you plan *your* menus, Nonni?" asked Olivia.

"Well," said Nonni Lidia. "I think about dishes that I love to make and eat and foods that are fresh that time of year. What are some foods *you* like to eat?"

"Raisins," said Olivia.

"French fries," said Lorenzo.

"Chocolate milk," said Miles.

"Pancakes," said Ethan.

"Pickles!" said Julia. "Lucia likes them too."

Nonni Lidia smiled and raised her eyebrows. "A supper of raisins, French fries, pancakes, chocolate milk, and pickles? Nonna Mima would certainly be surprised by that!"

The children giggled imagining the look on Nonna Mima's face.
"Maybe we'll be able to think better after a cookie break," said Nonni Lidia.
"Much better!" Ethan agreed.

"Did you help cook when you were a girl, Nonni?" asked Miles.

"Oh, not just cook," said Nonni Lidia. "I helped with every step of growing, gathering, and preparing the food too."

"Tell us more, Nonni Lidia!" said Olivia.

"Of course," said Nonni Lidia. "First we must go back to that very magical place—the courtyard of my grandparents' house. . . .

"As a girl, it was my enchanted little kingdom. There were hutches full of rabbits; pens of goats, geese, and chickens; and the pigsty. Roots, trees, and leafy greens grew in the rich soil, giving us fresh fruits and vegetables each new season.

"I can still see Nonna Rosa at her little stone smokehouse, its walls black from the smoke of the sausages, ham, and bacon she prepared there. It was happy, alive, and ever-changing. Each season brought its own special magic of colors, smells, and flavors.

"In the spring, we picked fresh, crisp peas in their shells. I plucked the tender little pearls from their pods until my fingers turned bright green—always popping a few in my mouth. *Mmmmm*, sweet as sugar!

"My brother, Franco, and I gathered clover and other flowers for the rabbits to eat. The bunnies thanked us by snuggling close and tickling our faces with their fur.

"The baby goats had just been born. All the spring flowers and grasses that the mama goats ate filled their milk with nutrients and flavor. The baby goats would suckle on the milk. I would also drink it, still warm from the just-milked mama goat. When there was enough milk, Nonna Rosa would use it to make her own ricotta cheese.

"In the summer, the air was full of bees, butterflies, and beautiful smells. The golden wheat was harvested, and Nonna would take bags of grain to the mill in batches. The miller ground it into fresh, silky flour. In exchange, Nonna Rosa would give him some of the flour.

"The warm sun turned the corn golden and the cherries ripe and oh-so sweet—nature's candy! Franco and I gladly picked them, playing while we worked—corn silk hair for Franco and dangly cherry earrings for me!

"I skipped around collecting eggs as the chickens and geese laid them. All the birds roamed free. The chickens were precise and laid their eggs in the nest. Nonna Rosa knew her chickens, and recognized immediately which one had laid an egg, just from the sound of its cluck. But those pesky geese laid eggs anywhere they pleased! I had to search everywhere.

"In the fall, many gifts of the land were ripe and ready for harvest. Nonna Rosa would preserve and save this food to feed us in the coldest months when nothing grew. We picked round, juicy grapes and hung some to dry from the ceiling. Do you know what they turned into? The best raisins I ever ate!

"We dug potatoes right out of the ground. I would hold them in my hands, still warm from the earth below, and wipe the dirt off them. Later, Nonna Rosa would roast them golden brown alongside a plump chicken topped with lots of rosemary.

"As winter neared, Nonna Rosa fattened up the pigs, feeding them well with table scraps—apple cores, potato peels—nothing went to waste. She cooked their food too, so it would be safe for their sensitive tummies!

"In the winter, the fields and the trees were barren. We relied on the foods
we had canned, cured, and preserved. Nonna Rosa always had a great stash of
tasty things—hanging sausages, bacon, hams, pickled vegetables, fruit jams,
dried beans, lentils, and bottles of olive oil lined up on a shelf like soldiers.
Our own little grocery store!

"There were also delicious dried fruits and nuts. We even used them to decorate our Christmas tree—a juniper bush cut fresh from the woods outside.

"On Christmas Day, Nonna Rosa always roasted a great big goose. I never liked geese much since they would always chase me around the courtyard honking in my face with their bright orange beaks. But I certainly loved them for Christmas dinner!

"This was life when I was a little girl—the cycle of food and nature would repeat every year, again and again. Each new year, while the earth was still too cold for growing, the fields were tilled and prepared for a new season of crops. New piglets and other animals were bought, and we waited patiently for spring to bring new color and life to the land. It was a very special way to live."

"I'll say!" said Olivia. "You even made your own *raisins*."

"That's so cool," said Miles.

"Did you guys make *everything* you ate?" asked Ethan.

"Almost everything," Nonni Lidia said. "Sometimes we went to the local market too.

"When we had more than we needed, Nonna Rosa would sell or trade our extra goods. This way, we could get other produce, meat, or fish that we didn't grow or make ourselves. Everything at the market was fresh and local—the best of each season.

"On market day, Nonna Rosa brought her special shopping cart. She would remind me of the rule:

> *Down the hill, you ride*
> *Up the hill, you push*

"I helped Nonna sell her goods and shop for what we needed. I loved to weigh the merchandise on the tipping scale. I knew when the scale needle pointed to twelve, the merchandise on one side equaled the weight on the other side of the scale."

Nonni Lidia looked at her grandchildren's faces and smiled.

"Will you take *us* to a market?" Olivia asked.

"We can see what's fresh and in season!" said Miles.

"Then we will be able to make our menu," said Lorenzo.

"I would love to!" said Nonni Lidia. "I know a wonderful farmer's market. Let me grab my cart!"

"Can I ride in it?" asked Julia.

"Maybe *down*hill," Nonni Lidia said, giving Julia a wink.

At the market, stalls overflowed with apricots and artichokes, mushrooms and spinach, rhubarb, radishes, strawberries, and onions. There were piles of potatoes dusted with dirt and carrots with green, frilly tops.

"Wow!" said Ethan. "It's a food rainbow!"

Nonni Lidia gave Olivia, Miles, Lorenzo, Ethan, and Julia each some money. "Pick something that looks and smells good to *you*," she said. "We can figure out what to make when we get it all home."

Olivia found tiny tomatoes in red and yellow.
"They're so cute!" she said. "They still have their little tops on them."
She breathed in their earthy, fragrant smell.

Miles saw a great big pile of green beans.
The man selling them snapped one in two and let Miles hear the crispy sound of a just-picked string bean.
"Wow," he said. The raw green bean was so crunchy and fresh-tasting.

A woman at a stall gave Julia a crate to stand on to look at the vegetables.
"I like these," said Julia. "They are like magic elf wands! *Ta-da!*"
"Asparagus," said Nonni Lidia. "Quite tasty roasted with a little salt and olive oil!"

Ethan saw a plate with little chunks of cheese. The man said he could sample as many as he wanted, so he did! "Mmmm! This one is so milky and delicious, let's take a piece home!" Ethan said.

The man cut him a small wedge of the Grana Padano cheese.

Lorenzo was in the next stall sniffing fresh herbs. He found one that smelled green and bright and just a tiny bit like licorice.

He pulled off a sprig and held it up to his nose. "Hey, Nonni," he said. "Look at my mustache!"

Nonni Lidia laughed. "I've never seen a *basil* mustache before!"

Back at Nonni Lidia's, the children stacked their ingredients on the counter. Nonni Lidia added some onion, garlic, and peas to the pile.

"How will we ever make one dinner with all of these different things?" Ethan asked.

Nonni Lidia smiled. "Ingredients are like members of a family," she said. "Each one is unique, and *together* they can make something quite special."

Nonni Lidia and the children got to work washing, chopping, stirring, boiling, and sautéing. They used cutting boards and colanders, pots, pans, knives, and spoons.

Olivia and Ethan were in charge of setting the table. They arranged flowers and a few artichokes from the market with some rosebuds from the yard.

At last everything was ready! Just in time, as their parents and Nonna Mima arrived.

"Happy Birthday, Nonna Mima!" the children shouted.

"We planned a meal for you," said Olivia.

"We even made our own menus!" said Lorenzo.

"It's pasta primavera," said Miles.

"That means spring!" said Ethan.

"Ta-Da!" said Julia.

The parents and Nonna Mima all cheered.

When they had finished eating, Nonna Mima raised her glass. "To the chefs!" she said. "Your Nonna Rosa would be very proud."

"To the chefs!" the parents and Nonni Lidia said.

Miles looked at Nonni Lidia. "So I guess that was better than raisins, French fries, pancakes, chocolate milk, and pickles?" he said.

Nonna Lidia thought for a minute. "Well," she said. "I'm not sure. Maybe if you all sleep over, we can make that for breakfast!"

Everyone laughed, including Nonni Lidia, who couldn't wait to have the whole family around the table enjoying another special meal they had planned and cooked together—the very best place to be in *any* season.

Spring Recipes

PASTA PRIMAVERA

You don't have to wait for *primavera*—springtime—to make this quick skillet sauce. You probably have most of the ingredients in your pantry and refrigerator all year: canned tomatoes; onions; garlic; a few perennially fresh vegetables like broccoli, mushrooms, and zucchini; and sweet peas from the freezer. This recipe lists the vegetables I prefer, but don't be afraid to use others, if that's what you have on hand.

Yield: Serves 6 to 8

6 quarts water for boiling plus a bowl of ice water

Vegetables, 3 cups in *total* of any of the following:

   Zucchini, sliced crosswise in ½-inch pieces

   Small broccoli florets on short stems, about 1-inch wide (slice if necessary)

   Green beans, trimmed and sliced on the bias in ¾-inch lengths

   Frozen sweet peas

   Asparagus, cut into 1-inch pieces

⅓ cup extra-virgin olive oil

½ cup onion, sliced

2 garlic cloves, crushed

1 (28-ounce) can San Marzano or other Italian plum tomatoes, with their juices, crushed by hand or 1½ cups of ripe cherry tomatoes, cut in half

1 pound spaghetti

½ teaspoon salt

4 basil leaves, shredded

½ cup Parmigiano-Reggiano cheese, grated

1. Bring 6 quarts of water to a boil in a large pot. In the meantime, prepare a bowl with ice water. When the pasta water is boiling, dump the 3 cups of vegetables in the boiling water. Bring the water back to a boil, and cook uncovered for 2 minutes. Scoop out the pieces with a spider or strainer, drain briefly, and drop into the ice water. When thoroughly chilled, drain them in a colander.

2. In the meantime, begin making the sauce. In a wide skillet with the olive oil, scatter the onion slices and crushed garlic cloves. Cook for 2 minutes over medium heat until the onions are wilted.

3. Pour the crushed tomatoes and juices into the skillet. Slosh the tomato can with 1 cup of water and add to the skillet (or add the cherry tomatoes). Bring all to a boil and let simmer for 5 minutes.

4. Drop the pasta into the boiling water while the sauce cooks.

5. Add the blanched vegetables to the skillet and stir them into the sauce, adding 1 cup of pasta water and ½ teaspoon of salt. Bring all to a simmer and cook for about 3 minutes or more, until the blanched vegetables are cooked thoroughly but still al dente. If too dry, add a little more pasta water.

6. Drain the pasta when cooked and add to the skillet with sauce. Toss in the shredded basil and toss all well. Drizzle the mixture with extra-virgin olive oil and let the pasta and sauce cook together for a few minutes.

7. When the pasta is well-coated with sauce, remove from the heat. Toss in the grated cheese and serve.

KIDS CAN:

Help choose their favorite vegetables; wash the vegetables; shred the basil; clean the garlic and onion; and add a little bit of freshly grated cheese before it goes to the table.

Rice and Pea Soup

Risi e Bisi

Everyone makes this classic soup a little differently, according to preference. I like my *risi e bisi* rather brothy while others make theirs quite dense. This is controlled by the intensity of the boil, using an open or covered pot, and cooking time, all of which determine the rate of evaporation. (I cook my soup covered, at a slow boil.)

Either long- or short-grain rice can be used here. Traditionally, the soup was made with short grain carnaroli or arborio rice, and I still think it produces the most authentic flavor and texture. Short-grain rice cooks faster, but if you need to cook the soup longer or reheat it, the rice tends to dissolve. Long-grain rice, on the other hand, stays more intact in a long-cooking or reheated soup.

Yield: 3 quarts, serves 8

3 tablespoons extra-virgin olive oil plus more for serving

¼ pound bacon (about 4 thick-cut strips), cut crosswise in ⅓-inch pieces

2 cups leeks, diced in ½-inch pieces (about 6 ounces)

3 cups peas or edamame, fresh, shucked (or 1 pound frozen)

3 quarts water

1 tablespoon plus ½ teaspoon coarse sea salt or kosher salt or to taste

¾ to 1 cup long-grain rice

4 tablespoons fresh Italian parsley, chopped

Freshly grated Grana Padano for serving

Freshly ground black pepper to taste

1. Pour the olive oil in the heavy pot and set over medium heat. Stir in the bacon pieces and cook for several minutes to render the fat. When the bacon starts to crisp, stir in the leeks (and fresh peas, if using). Cook, stirring frequently, until the leeks are wilted and the bacon is caramelized, about 6 minutes.

2. Meanwhile heat 3 quarts of water to a simmer. Pour into the pot with the onions and bacon, add the tablespoon of salt, and stir well. Rapidly bring to a boil, then adjust the heat to maintain active bubbling. Cook for an hour, covered, to build flavor in the soup base.

3. If using frozen peas, add now, return the soup to a bubbling simmer, and cook for 20 minutes before adding the rice. (If fresh peas are already cooking in the pot, stir in the rice after the hour or so of cooking.) Use ¾ cup rice for a looser soup or a full cup of rice for a denser one and add to the soup. Return the soup to an active simmer, taste, and stir in ½ teaspoon or more of salt—remember that more rice needs more seasoning.

4. Cook the rice for 10 minutes or so, stirring occasionally, until the grains are cooked through but not mushy. Turn off the heat, stir in the parsley and grated cheese; season the soup with lots of freshly ground black pepper. Serve immediately, passing more cheese and olive oil at the table.

KIDS CAN:

Measure out the ingredients; clean and wash the leeks; pick the parsley leaves for chopping; shuck the peas or edamame if fresh; and add grated cheese.

Sausage and Bread Frittata

Frittata is the quintessential Italian meal. You can flavor it with anything you have on hand, and one of my favorite ways is adding day-old bread with vegetables and sausages. When there is nothing else in the house except eggs, this is the meal to make.

Yield: Serves 4 to 6

3 tablespoons extra-virgin olive oil

8 ounces sweet Italian sausage, removed from casing (about 2 links)

½ cup onion, chopped

1 cup shredded zucchini

8 large eggs

½ teaspoon kosher salt

¼ cup milk (whole or low fat)

1½ cups day-old country bread, cut into ½-inch cubes

½ cup Grana Padano or Parmigiano-Reggiano, grated

1. Preheat oven to 375°F.

2. Heat oil in a 9-inch nonstick skillet over medium heat. Add sausages and cook until crisp, about 5 to 6 minutes. Push sausage to one side of the skillet, and add onions and shredded zucchini. Cook until wilted, then mix in the sausages. Continue to cook while you prepare the eggs and the bread.

3. In a bowl, beat eggs with the salt, add milk, and toss in the bread cubes. Let it soak for 3 to 4 minutes.

4. Reduce heat to medium, add the egg bread mixture, quickly stir, and then let cook until the eggs begin to set around the edges of the pan, about 2 to 3 minutes, without stirring.

5. Sprinkle all over with the grated cheese. Bake frittata in the oven until set all the way through and the top is golden, about 12 minutes.

6. Run a knife around the edge of the skillet, let rest for 10 minutes, and invert onto a plate or cutting board. Serve in wedges, warm or at room temperature.

KIDS CAN:

Tear bread; count the eggs; and help crack and beat the eggs with the salt and milk.

PANNA COTTA WITH BERRIES

Yield: Serves 6

1½ cups heavy cream

1½ cups whole milk, divided

1½ cups sugar, divided

1 vanilla bean, split lengthwise

1 orange, peel removed with a
   vegetable peeler, juiced

1 tablespoon powdered gelatin

2 cups ripe strawberries, washed
   and quartered

1 cup blueberries, washed

Few sprigs of mint (optional)

1. Bring the cream, 1 cup milk, ¾ cup sugar, the vanilla bean, and orange peel to a boil. Remove from the heat and cool to room temperature.

2. Sprinkle gelatin over remaining ½ cup milk and let sit 5 minutes.

3. Whisk ½ cup sugar and gelatin mixture into cream mixture over medium heat. Whisk until gelatin and sugar dissolve and mixture just comes to a simmer. Scrape vanilla bean seeds into the pot, and then strain mixture through a fine sieve into a large spouted measuring cup.

4. Pour into six (4- or 5-ounce) ramekins. Chill in the refrigerator until set, 6 hours or overnight.

5. In the meantime, combine strawberries, blueberries, remaining ¼ cup sugar, and the orange juice in a bowl. Refrigerate to blend flavors, about an hour.

6. Unmold the panna cotta by passing a paring knife around the inside rim of the mold and transfer all the panna cotta on individual serving plates, upside down. Spoon the marinated berries over the panna cotta. Add sprigs of mint for decoration and serve.

NOTE: If the panna cotta does not unmold right away, dip the ramekin in hot water for a few seconds to loosen it and try again.

KIDS CAN:

Measure the ingredients; wash the berries; mix the strawberries, blueberries, sugar, and orange juice
in a bowl; unmold the panna cotta; spoon the marinated berries over the panna cotta;
and decorate with the sprigs of mint.

Summer Recipes

BREAD AND TOMATO SALAD

Yield: Serves 6

1 pound two-day-old country-style bread, crusts removed, cut into ½-inch cubes (about 8 cups)

2 pounds ripe tomatoes at room temperature, cored, seeded, and cut into ½-inch cubes (about 4 cups)

1 cup red onion, sliced

12 fresh basil leaves, shredded

5 tablespoons extra-virgin olive oil

3 tablespoons red wine vinegar

Salt and freshly ground black pepper

Fresh basil sprigs

In a large bowl, toss bread, tomatoes, onion, and shredded basil leaves until well mixed. Drizzle the olive oil and vinegar over the salad, and toss to mix thoroughly. Season to taste with salt and pepper, and let stand 10 minutes before serving. Decorate with sprigs of fresh basil.

KIDS CAN:

Pull basil leaves off the stems and shred them; grind pepper; toss the ingredients in the large bowl, and mix; and measure the oil and vinegar to dress the salad.

QUICK MARINARA SAUCE WITH ZITI AND MOZZARELLA CUBES

Yield: Makes about 3½ cups,
enough to sauce 6 servings of pasta

6 quarts water

Salt

¼ cup extra-virgin olive oil

8 garlic cloves, peeled
and crushed

3 pounds ripe fresh plum
tomatoes, peeled and seeded
or 1 (28-ounce) can of peeled
Italian tomatoes, seeded and
lightly crushed, with their liquid

2 sprigs of fresh basil

Peperoncino
(crushed red pepper) to taste

1 pound ziti

2 cups fresh mozzarella,
cut into ½-inch cubes

½ cup Grana Padano, grated

½ cup fresh basil leaves,
loosely packed and shredded,
for garnish (optional)

1. Bring a pot with 6 quarts of salted water to a boil.

2. In a medium-size, nonreactive saucepan, heat the olive oil over medium heat. Add the garlic and cook until lightly browned, about 2 minutes.

3. Carefully add the tomatoes and their liquid. Add the basil sprigs, bring to a boil, and season lightly with salt and crushed red pepper. About 10 minutes after the sauce has been on the stove, throw the ziti in the boiling water to cook. Reduce the heat to a simmer and break up the tomatoes with a whisk as they cook, until the sauce is chunky and thick, about 20 minutes. Taste the sauce and add salt and pepper if necessary.

4. Remove the basil sprigs and garlic cloves.

5. Drain ziti and add to simmering sauce; toss well until pasta is coated with sauce. Turn off the stove, toss in mozzarella cubes and grated cheese, and serve immediately, topping with some shredded fresh basil leaves if desired.

KIDS CAN:

Separate and peel garlic cloves; add mozzarella cubes; toss in grated cheese;
and mix and help garnish the dish with basil leaves.

Tomato Almond Pesto
with Spaghetti

The beauty and delight of this dish is that it is so fresh and clean—and it is a cinch to make. It is important to make the pesto with the best ingredients. Once it is ready, just toss it in a bowl with some hot, cooked spaghetti and enjoy!

Yield: Serves 4 to 6

¾ pound (about 2½ cups) cherry tomatoes, very ripe and sweet

12 large fresh basil leaves

2 plump garlic cloves, crushed and peeled

⅓ cup of whole almonds, lightly toasted

¼ teaspoon peperoncino or to taste

1 tablespoon plus ½ teaspoon coarse sea salt or kosher salt, or to taste, plus more for the pasta

½ cup extra-virgin olive oil

1 pound spaghetti

½ cup Parmigiano-Reggiano or Grana Padano, freshly grated

1. Rinse the cherry tomatoes and pat them dry. Rinse the basil leaves and pat them dry.

2. Drop the tomatoes into the blender jar or food processor bowl, followed by the garlic cloves, almonds, basil leaves, peperoncino, and ½ teaspoon sea or kosher salt. Blend for a minute or more to a fine purée; scrape down the bowl and blend again if any large bits or pieces have survived.

3. While the machine is running, pour in the olive oil in a steady stream, emulsifying the purée into a thick pesto. Taste and adjust seasoning. (If you're going dress the pasta within a couple of hours, leave the pesto at room temperature. Refrigerate for longer storage, up to 2 days, but let it return to room temperature before cooking the pasta.)

4. To cook the spaghetti, heat 6 quarts of water with 1 tablespoon salt to a boil in the large pot. Scrape all the pesto into a big warm bowl.

5. Cook the spaghetti al dente, lift it from the cooking pot, drain briefly, and drop onto the pesto. Toss quickly to coat the spaghetti, adding a ladle or two of the pasta cooking water if needed. Sprinkle the cheese all over, and toss again. Serve immediately in warm bowls.

KIDS CAN:

Wash the cherry tomatoes and basil and pat them dry; spoon the pesto into the cooked pasta; toss the pasta to coat with pesto; and add the grated cheese.

RIPE PEACHES, CHERRY, AND MINT SOUP

Yield: Serves 12

10 ripe peaches,
   peeled and sliced

½ cup sugar

2 cups fresh orange juice

Juice of 2 lemons

1 cup seltzer water

30 mint leaves, torn into pieces

1 pint ripe cherries,
   pitted and halved

Mix the sliced peaches with sugar in a large bowl. Mix orange and lemon juices with the seltzer water, and pour over the peaches. Add half the mint leaves and allow the mixture to marinate in the refrigerator for 20 minutes. Stir in the cherries, and garnish with the remaining mint.

KIDS CAN:

Juice the oranges and lemons; measure and mix the sugar in with the peaches;
stir juices, seltzer water, and fruit together in a bowl; pick and tear mint leaves and then use
half of them to garnish; and pit the cherries.

CHICKEN SOUP WITH PASTINA

Brodo di Pollo con Pastina

Free-range chickens make superior stock. I also like the richness that turkey wings add to a chicken stock, so I use them all the time. You can save the chicken parts you need for stock over time. Keep them in a sealable bag or container in the freezer, or perhaps your butcher can sell you what you need. Remove the livers from the giblet bag before making stock—livers will add a bitter flavor.

Yield: 3½ quarts, serves 10 to 12

3 pounds chicken and/or turkey wings, backs, necks, and giblets (not including the liver), preferably from free-range or organically raised birds

8 quarts water

1 large onion (about ½ pound), cut in half

3 cups carrots, peeled and sliced 1-inch thick

3 celery stalks, cut crosswise into 4 pieces

6 garlic cloves

6 sprigs fresh Italian parsley

6 whole black peppercorns

1 tablespoon salt

Rind of Grana Padano or Parmigiano-Reggiano cheese (scraped and washed)

½ cup to 1 cup pastina for 1 quart of cooked soup

Freshly grated Grana Padano or Parmigiano-Reggiano for serving

1. Wash the chicken parts and/or turkey wings thoroughly under cold running water, and drain them well. Put them with the water in a large stockpot, and bring to a boil over high heat. Lower heat to medium, and simmer for 1 hour. Skim off the surface foam and fat occasionally.

2. Add to the pot all the remaining ingredients except the pastina and cheese for serving. Bring the pot to a boil again, occasionally skimming the fat and foam off the top. Lower the heat until the liquid is "perking"—one or two large bubbles rising to the surface at a time. Partially cover and cook for 2 hours, adding salt to taste, about 1 tablespoon in all. When the solids are cool, pick out the carrot pieces and bones from the pieces of meat. Set aside to be added to soup when served.

3. Strain the soup through a fine strainer and/or cheese cloth.

4. Let set and de-fat the soup.

5. When ready to serve, bring one quart of soup or more to a boil. Add the pastina and bring to a boil, about 3 to 4 minutes, and taste the pastina for doneness. Add the carrots and chicken pieces if desired, and serve with grated Grana Padano or Parmigiano-Reggiano.

NOTE: If you'd like to keep some soup for later, just freeze without the pastina for future use.

KIDS CAN:

Clean the onion and garlic; pull celery stalks off; and strain the cool stock.

ROASTED SWEET POTATOES
WITH THYME

Patate Dolci al Forno con Timo

Everybody loves roasted potatoes, and these have a Mediterranean twist with lots of garlic and rosemary. The aroma of roasted potatoes conjures up images of big roasted meats and holidays, so whenever I make this dish it feels like a holiday to me.

Yield: Serves 4 to 6

¼ cup plus 3 tablespoons extra-virgin olive oil

2 tablespoons fresh thyme leaves, chopped

4 garlic cloves, sliced

2 pounds sweet potatoes, peeled and cut into ½-inch pieces

1 teaspoon kosher salt

1. Preheat oven to 425°F.

2. In a large bowl, combine ¼ cup of the olive oil, thyme, and garlic. Throw in the cut-up sweet potatoes, season with salt, and let steep for 30 minutes.

3. Spread potatoes on a rimmed baking sheet brushed with the remaining 3 tablespoons olive oil. Roast until golden on one side, about 15 minutes. Flip with a spatula and roast until golden on the other side and potatoes are cooked through and very crispy, about 15 minutes more.

4. Serve immediately. You can pick out some or all of the garlic before serving if you like.

KIDS CAN:

Pick the thyme leaves for chopping; clean the garlic; toss thyme and garlic with olive oil; spread potatoes on a baking sheet; season with salt; and brush potatoes with olive oil.

CRISPY BAKED TURKEY CUTLETS

I make a platter of these crumb-coated baked morsels for the kids when they come over because I know they will enjoy them and be nourished. But I notice most of the adults take a piece too. The cutlets have the crunchy appeal of fast-food style fried "nuggets" and "fingers," but they are better in every way.

Yield: Serves 6 or more if serving small eaters under 4 years of age

2 pounds turkey breast cutlets or "tenders," or skinless, boneless chicken breasts

¼ teaspoon salt

3 plump garlic cloves, sliced

3 tablespoons extra-virgin olive oil plus more for drizzling on the cutlets

1 to 2 tablespoons unsalted butter (for the baking sheet)

Cheesy Crumbs

½ cup dried bread crumbs

¾ cup Parmigiano-Reggiano or Grana Padano, freshly grated

2 tablespoons fresh Italian parsley, chopped

2 tablespoons extra-virgin olive oil

¼ teaspoon salt

KIDS CAN:

Help pound turkey cutlets; blend together the ingredients for cheesy bread crumbs; butter the baking sheet; coat the cutlets in breadcrumbs (be sure to wash your hands carefully after touching the raw meat!) by tossing the strips in the bowl and patting them so the bread crumbs stick; and place the breaded tenders on the buttered baking sheet.

1. Rinse and dry the breast pieces and trim off all fat and tendons. Slice the meat (with the grain rather than across it) in strips roughly 2 inches wide and 4 inches long: you should get 10 to 15 pieces. Pound thick or uneven pieces, if necessary, with a meat mallet or other heavy flat object so they are an even $^1/_2$- to $^2/_3$-inch thick.

2. Put the strips in a bowl and toss them with the salt, garlic slices, and olive oil. Let them marinate for at least 15 minutes, though preferably 30 minutes, at room temperature.

3. Meanwhile, set a rack in the upper third of the oven—nearer to the top for browning—and heat it to 425°F.

4. Toss and stir together the bread crumbs, grated cheese, parsley, 2 tablespoons of olive oil, and $^1/_4$ teaspoon of salt until thoroughly blended. Lightly butter the baking sheet.

5. When the meat has marinated, lift out a few pieces and pick off the garlic slices. Drop the strips in the crumbs and roll them around, then pick them up one by one and press the crumbs so they stick to the meat on both sides. Try a one-hand technique: scoop up a turkey strip and crumbs in the palm of your hand, then close your fingers and squeeze tight.

6. Lay the coated strips flat on the baking sheet spaced at least a $^1/_4$ inch apart. If you see bare spots of meat, press on a few of the remaining crumbs. Drizzle a bit more olive oil on each strip and put the pan in the oven.

7. Bake for 8 minutes. Rotate the sheet back to the front, and bake for another 8 minutes or until the crumbs are golden brown on top and the meat is cooked through but still moist. Cut a piece open to check doneness. If the crumbs are browning quickly while the meat is still uncooked, set the tray lower in the oven and/or lay a sheet of foil on top of the cutlets. Don't let them overcook, and move them to a platter as soon as they come out of the oven so they don't dry out on the hot baking sheet.

8. Serve hot or warm. They are still very good reheated and make great sandwiches.

CARROT AND APPLE SALAD

Here's another fine winter salad. This one is made of crunchy carrots and fresh seasonal apples. The crunchy complexity of the carrots and the crisp apple provide a delightful, unexpected combination of flavor and texture. To turn the salad into a light lunch, add a few slices of prosciutto and serve it with some crusty bread.

A firm, crisp apple is what you want for salad, and fortunately there are many varieties in the market that have that essential crunch, with flavors ranging from sweet to tangy to tart. I like to use a few different apples for greater complexity of flavor and vivid color in the salad. In addition to the reliably crisp Granny Smith apple, I look for some of the old-time firm and tart apples, such as Gravenstein, Jonathan, and Rome.

Yield: Serves 6

1 pound firm, crisp apples
(see above for varieties)

1 pound of firm organic
carrots, peeled

2 tablespoons cider vinegar

1 tablespoon Dijon mustard

1½ teaspoons kosher salt

Freshly ground black pepper
to taste

¼ cup extra-virgin olive oil

⅓ cup chopped chives (optional)

1. Rinse the apples well, but don't peel them. Slice them in half, through the stem and bottom ends, and cut out the seeds and cores. Set in a food processor equipped with a blade to cut in matchsticks, and cut the apples and carrots.

2. Add the apples and carrots to the bowl and gently toss them together.

3. For the dressing: Whisk together the vinegar, mustard, salt, and pepper in a small bowl, and then whisk in the olive oil gradually, until smooth and emulsified.

4. Pour the dressing over the carrots and apples, and toss to coat all the slices with dressing. Sprinkle with chopped chives (optional).

5. Serve cold or at room temperature.

KIDS CAN:

Rinse the apples; toss apples and carrots together in a bowl; grind the pepper; help measure and whisk together dressing ingredients and then dress the salad; and sprinkle the chives.

LENTILS AND DITALINI PASTA

Yield: 3 quarts, serves 8 to 10

¼ cup extra-virgin olive oil

1½ pounds russet potatoes, peeled and diced into ½-inch cubes (4 cups)

2 teaspoons salt, divided, plus more to balance the pasta

2 celery stalks, finely chopped (about 1½ cups)

2 medium carrots, peeled and grated (about 1½ cups)

3 tablespoons tomato paste

5 quarts water

3 whole bay leaves

1 or 2 pieces outer rind of Parmigiano-Reggiano or Grana Padano (2- or 3-inch squares), rinsed

2 cup lentils, rinsed and picked over

2 cup ditalini or other short tubular pasta

Freshly ground black pepper

Freshly grated Parmigiano-Reggiano or Grana Padano cheese for serving

1. Pour the oil into the pot and set over medium-high heat. Let the oil get quite hot, but not smoking.

2. Add in the potatoes, sprinkle in 1 teaspoon of the salt, and toss them in the oil until well coated. Cook them for 6 minutes or more, until lightly crusted and caramelized without taking on any color. Lower the heat to prevent burning and alternately stir the potatoes.

3. When the potatoes leave a crust on the pan bottom (about 3 to 5 minutes), toss in the celery and carrots. Stir up everything well, scraping up any potato crust, raise the heat a bit, and cook for 2 or 3 minutes, until all the vegetables are hot and steaming. Push them aside to clear the pan bottom in the center and drop in the tomato paste. Toast it in the hot spot for a minute or two, stirring, and then work the paste into the vegetables.

4. Pour the water into the pan, drop in the bay leaves and pieces of cheese rind, add another teaspoon of salt, and stir well. Cover the pot and bring the broth to a boil, adjusting the heat to keep a steady but not violent bubbling, and let cook for an hour. Stir occasionally.

5. Add the lentils to the pot and cook the broth for another 30 minutes at a low bubbling boil. Remove the bay leaves but leave the cheese rind, whole or chopped up, for those who like it.

6. Taste and add more salt to balance the pasta; stir in the ditalini and cook for 12 minutes or more, until the pasta is to your liking. Add hot water to thin the soup, if necessary. Add pepper and adjust the seasoning one last time and serve right away in warm bowls, with freshly grated cheese.

KIDS CAN:

Peel potatoes and carrots (with adult supervision); measure and add tomato paste; measure and add lentils and pasta; and add grated cheese.

SAVORY POTATO BROTH

This versatile soup base is not truly a broth in the way my turkey broth is—that is, a clear liquid strained of all the ingredients that give it flavor. In truth, the base starts cooking with several pounds of potatoes, carrots, and celery, and they stay in there. Remarkably, it ends up light, clear, and clean tasting, so the word broth seems to fit.

Yield: 4 quarts of soup, serves 10 to 12

¼ cup extra-virgin olive oil

2½ pounds russet potatoes, peeled and diced into ½-inch cubes (6 cups)

2 teaspoons salt, divided

2 celery stalks, finely chopped (about 1½ cups)

2 medium carrots, peeled and grated (about 1½ cups)

3 tablespoons tomato paste

6 quarts water, heated to boiling

3 whole bay leaves

1 or 2 pieces outer rind of Parmigiano-Reggiano or Grana Padano (2- or 3-inch squares), rinsed

¼ teaspoon freshly ground black pepper or more to taste

2 cups long-grain rice

Freshly grated Parmigiano-Reggiano or Grana Padano cheese for serving

1. Pour the oil into the pot and set over medium-high heat. Let the oil get quite hot, but not smoking.

2. Add in the potatoes, sprinkle in 1 teaspoon of the salt, and toss them in the oil until well coated. Cook them for 6 minutes or more, until lightly crusted and caramelized without taking on any color. Lower the heat to prevent burning and alternately stir the potatoes.

3. When the potatoes leave a crust on the pan bottom (about 3 to 5 minutes), toss in the celery and carrots. Stir up everything well, scraping up any potato crust, raise the heat a bit, and cook for 2 or 3 minutes, until all the vegetables are hot and steaming. Push them aside to clear the pan bottom in the center and drop in the tomato paste. Toast it in the hot spot for a minute or two, stirring, then work the paste into the vegetables.

4. Pour the 6 quarts of hot water into the pan, drop in the bay leaves and pieces of cheese rind, grind in $1/4$ teaspoon or more of black pepper, add another teaspoon of salt, and stir well. Cover the pot and bring the broth to a boil, adjusting the heat to keep a steady but not violent bubbling and let cook for an hour, covered. Stir occasionally.

5. Uncover the pot and cook the broth for another 45 minutes or so, still at a low bubbling boil, until it has reduced to 4 quarts. Add the rice and cook for an additional 12 to 15 minutes until the rice is cooked.

6. Remove the bay leaves but leave the cheese rind, whole or chopped up, for those who like it.

7. Serve hot with grated cheese.

KIDS CAN:

Wash the celery and carrots; measure the tomato paste and rice; and add grated cheese.

POTATO GNOCCHI
WITH BUTTER SAGE SAUCE

Yield: Serves 6

2 large pots of water, divided
(1 for boiling potatoes and
1 for cooking gnocchi)

1½ pounds baking potatoes

¾ teaspoon salt

1 large egg, beaten well

1½ to 2 cups all-purpose flour,
divided

For this recipe, you will need a
potato ricer or vegetable mill.

Making and Shaping the Gnocchi

1. Boil the potatoes in water and cover until tender when poked with a fork. Don't let them overcook to the point that their skins split. Drain.

2. As soon as the potatoes are cool enough to handle, peel them and put them through the ricer or vegetable mill, using the medium disk and letting the shreds fall onto a large baking tray or board. Spread them out, sprinkle on the salt, and let them dry out and cool for at least 20 minutes.

3. Pour the beaten egg over the potatoes and then 1 cup of the flour. Gather the mass together and knead, adding a little more flour as necessary to make the dough hold together. But keep it light; the more you work the dough, the more flour you'll need, and you don't want to incorporate too much or the gnocchi will be heavy and dry. A good criterion: Slice the mass in half and examine the texture. It should look like cookie dough peppered with small holes.

4. Cut the dough into 3 equal pieces. Roll out each portion into a broomstick about 18 inches long, then cut crosswise into ²/₃-inch pieces and toss them lightly in flour. You should have about 72 gnocchi.

5. Take one piece of gnocchi and place it cut-side-down on the tines of a fork. Then with your lightly floured thumb, press into it, at the same time pushing it off the end of the fork and onto a floured board. The gnocchi should have an indentation where your thumb was and ridges from the fork tines on the other side. Repeat with all the remaining pieces and cover with a clean towel. At this point they should be cooked immediately or quickly frozen.

KIDS CAN:

Help rice potatoes and knead, shape, and cut gnocchi dough.

Cooking the Gnocchi

1. Bring a large pot of salted water to a boil.

2. Drop the gnocchi, 5 or 6 at a time, into a large pot of boiling, salted water—the larger the pot the less time they will take to return to the boil.

3. Once they have cooked for 2 to 3 minutes, they will plump up and float to the surface. Fish them out with a strainer or slotted spoon, and drop them gently from your strainer into the waiting sauce.

Butter and Fresh Sage Sauce

Yield: For 1 Recipe of Gnocchi

12 tablespoons (1½ sticks) unsalted butter, to taste

12 fresh whole sage leaves

1 cup hot water from the pasta cooking pot

¼ teaspoon freshly ground black pepper or to taste

1 cup Parmigiano-Reggiano or Grana Padano, grated

1. Melt the butter in the pan over medium heat, lay in the sage leaves, and heat until the butter is sizzling gently. Toast the leaves for 1 minute or so.

2. Ladle in 1 cup boiling pasta water; stir the sauce and simmer for about 2 minutes.

3. Grind the black pepper directly into the sauce.

4. Keep the sauce hot over very low heat; return to a simmer just before adding gnocchi.

5. Drain gnocchi and add to the sauce in the skillet. Toss gently until all gnocchi are coated with sauce. Off the heat, toss in the cheese just before serving.

Italian American Meatloaf with Garlic Mashed Potatoes

Yield: Serves 10 or more

Italian American Meatloaf

2 cups day-old country-style
   bread, cut into cubes with crust

1 cup whole milk

2 medium carrots, cut in chunks

2 medium celery stalks,
   cut in chunks

1 medium onion, cut in chunks

1½ pounds ground beef

1½ pounds ground pork

1 bunch scallions,
   trimmed and chopped

1 cup Parmigiano-Reggiano
   or Grana Padano, grated

1 cup marinara sauce
   or puréed canned tomatoes

½ cup fresh Italian parsley,
   chopped

2 teaspoons kosher salt

1 teaspoon dry oregano

2 tablespoons extra-virgin
   olive oil

1. Preheat oven to 375°F. Put bread cubes in a medium bowl and pour the milk over. Let soak until bread is soft. Meanwhile, in a food processor, combine the carrot, celery, and onion, and pulse to make a fine-textured paste or *pestata*.

2. When the bread is soft, squeeze out the excess milk and put the bread in a large mixing bowl. Add *pestata*, ground meats, scallions, grated cheese, marinara sauce, parsley, salt, and oregano. Mix well with your hands to evenly distribute all of the ingredients. Oil a 15-by-10 Pyrex® (or other) baking dish with the olive oil. Form meat mixture into a loaf in the oiled pan.

3. Bake until brown and cooked through (the center of the meatloaf should read 165°F in an instant read thermometer), about 1 hour and 15 minutes. Let cool for 10 minutes before slicing.

KIDS CAN:

Pour milk over the breadcrumbs; squeeze milk out of the bread mixture; and add the ingredients and help mix with hands. (Be sure to wash hands carefully after touching raw meat!)

Olive Oil Mashed Potatoes

Purea di Patate all'Olio d'Oliva

Try this recipe for a delicious Italian rendition of mashed potatoes. I recall that my grandma would fork-mash boiled potatoes, drizzle some extra-virgin olive oil, and sprinkle with coarse sea salt. Here I added some roasted garlic cloves—very much an Italian-American favorite.

Yield: Serves 4 to 6

2 garlic heads

¼ cup extra-virgin olive oil, plus more for drizzling garlic heads

2 teaspoons kosher salt

1 large pot of water

2½ pounds medium russet potatoes

1 cup whole milk

1. Preheat oven to 375°F. Cut the tips of the garlic heads off so each garlic clove is slightly exposed. Place each garlic head on a square of foil, drizzle with olive oil, and wrap the foil to seal. Roast in oven until garlic is tender throughout, about 30 to 40 minutes, depending on the size of the garlic head. Let cool slightly, then squeeze roasted garlic head from the bottom so the cloves come out and set them into a small bowl. Mash the roasted garlic cloves with the ¼ cup of olive oil and salt.

2. Meanwhile, put the potatoes in a pot with water to cover them by 1 inch. Bring to a simmer and cook until tender all the way through. Drain, let cool slightly and then peel. In the pot used to cook the potatoes, warm the milk over low heat. Add the potatoes and garlic paste. Coarsely mash with a potato masher and serve hot.

KIDS CAN:

Wrap garlic heads in foil, and mash garlic and/or potatoes.

CHOCOLATE BREAD PARFAIT

This recipe recalls for me the chocolate-and-bread sandwiches that sometimes were my lunch, and always a special treat. And it is another inventive way surplus is used in Umbrian cuisine, with leftover country-style bread serving as the foundation of an elegant layered dessert. Although it is soaked with chocolate sauce and buried in whipped cream, the bread doesn't disintegrate. It serves as a pleasing textural contrast in every heavenly spoonful.

Yield: Serves 6

8 ounces bittersweet
   or semisweet chocolate,
   finely chopped

Pan of water

8 ounces country-style white
   bread, crusts removed

1 cup hot chocolate

1 teaspoon vanilla

1½ cups heavy cream, chilled

2 tablespoons sugar

1 cup almonds, sliced and toasted

1. Put the chopped chocolate in a bowl set in a pan of hot (not boiling) water. When the chocolate begins to melt, stir until completely smooth. Keep it warm, over the water, off the heat.

2. Slice the bread into ½-inch-thick slices, and lay them flat in one layer, close together, on the tray or baking sheet.

3. Pour the hot chocolate and vanilla into a spouted measuring cup, mix well, and then stir in half the melted chocolate.

4. Pour the sauce all over the bread slices, then flip them over and turn them on the tray to make sure all the surfaces are coated. Let the bread absorb the sauce for a few minutes.

5. Meanwhile, whip the cream with the sugar until soft peaks form, by hand or with an electric mixer.

To Assemble the Parfaits

1. Break the bread into 1-inch pieces. Use half the pieces to make the bottom parfait layer in the six serving glasses, placing an equal amount of chocolatey bread into each.

2. Drop a layer of whipped cream in the glasses, drizzle with some of the melted chocolate, and sprinkle with some toasted almonds.

3. Repeat the layering sequence: drop more soaked bread into each glass, and drizzle the chocolate sauce from the tray and the remaining melted chocolate over it.

4. Dollop another layer of whipped cream in the glasses, using it all up, and sprinkle the remaining almonds on top of each parfait. This dessert is best when served immediately while the melted chocolate is still warm and runny.

KIDS CAN:

Measure ingredients; lay out the bread on the baking sheet; pour the sauce all over the bread slices; whip the cream and sugar (though adults should help); break the bread into 1-inch pieces and layer with chocolate sauce and whipped cream in the glasses; and sprinkle the toasted almonds.